Hide-and-Seek in The Castle

BACK PACK BOOKS

NEW YORK

Knock, knock.
Bert and Buster arrive at
the castle. They have been
invited to a party.

Basil the Butler opens
the heavy wooden door.
"Good evening," he says.
"Please come inside."

Can you spot Basil the Butler
in the other pictures
in this book?

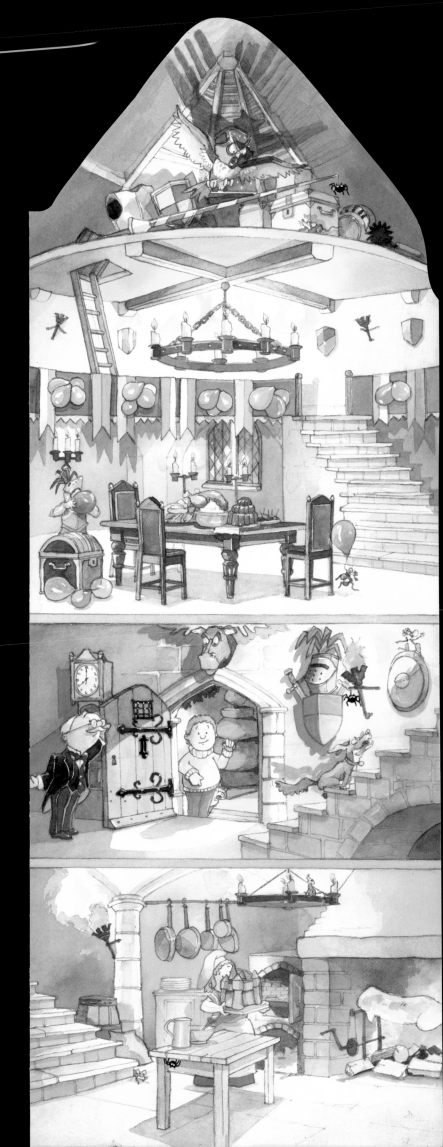

Yum, yum.
Bert and Buster look at all
the delicious party food.

But nobody has noticed
Kitty the Cat sneaking
into the castle. She wants
to join in the fun.

Can you find Kitty the Cat
in the other pictures
in this book?

Squish, squelch.
Oh dear, Kitty the Cat has
knocked over the pudding,
and now she is covered in it.

In the kitchen, Cassie the Cook
is making a beautiful cake
in the shape of a castle.

Can you see the castle-shaped
cake in the other pictures
in this book?

Pop, bang.
At the party, there are
balloons to play with.
But Buster pops his green balloon.
A bold mouse has taken a red
balloon, and floats around the
castle holding on to it.

Can you spot the mouse with
the red balloon in the other
pictures in this book?

Whoo, whoo.
Oliver the Owl says hello
to Bert and Buster.

He is sitting on a perch in the
attic at the top of the castle.
Oliver wants to come to
the party.

Can you see Oliver the Owl
in the other pictures
in this book?

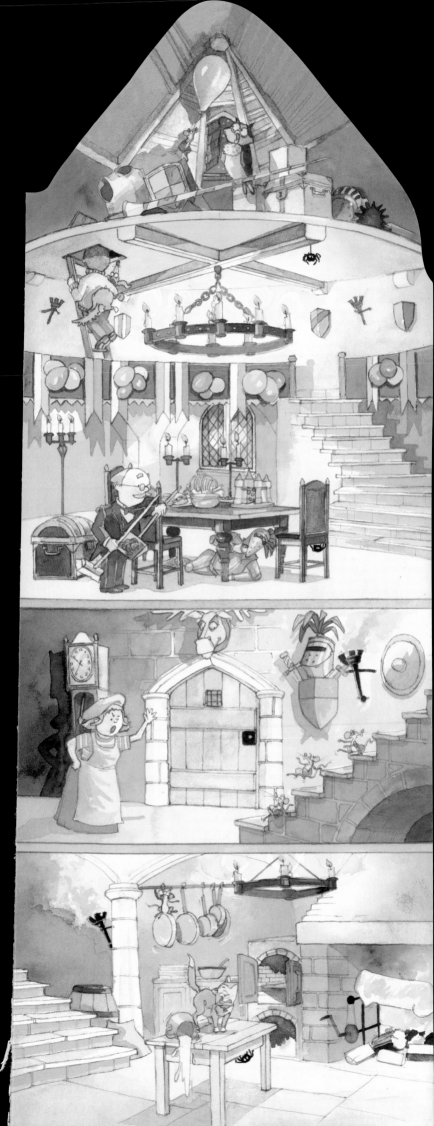

Clink, clank.
Here comes someone
wearing a suit of armor.

Look! It's Rollo. He lives
in the castle, and it is his party.
"Welcome everyone," he says.
"Let's play hide-and-seek."

Can you spot Rollo wearing his
suit of armor in the other
pictures in this book?